Little Whistle's
Christmas

CYNTHIA RYLANT

Illustrated by TIM BOWERS

Harcourt, Inc.

Orlando   Austin   New York   San Diego   Toronto   London

To Karrie
—C. R.

To Alice and Ron
—T. B.

Text copyright © 2003 by Cynthia Rylant
Illustrations copyright © 2003 by Tim Bowers

Requests for permission to make copies of any part of the work
should be mailed to the following address: Permissions Department,
Harcourt, Inc., 6277 Sea Harbor Drive, Orlando, Florida 32887-6777.

www.HarcourtBooks.com

Library of Congress Cataloging-in-Publication Data
Rylant, Cynthia.
Little Whistle's Christmas/Cynthia Rylant; illustrated by Tim Bowers.
p. cm.
Summary: Little Whistle, a real guinea pig who lives in a store called
Toytown, helps his toy friends write a letter to Santa asking if he made them.
[1. Toys—Fiction. 2. Guinea pigs—Fiction. 3. Santa Claus—Fiction.
4. Christmas—Fiction.] I. Bowers, Tim, ill. II. Title.
PZ7.R982Lje 2003
[E]—dc21   2002012211
ISBN 0-15-204590-2

First edition
H G F E D C B A
Manufactured in Mexico

The illustrations in this book were done in oil paint on canvas.
The display type was set in Minister.
The text type was set in Goudy Catalogue.
Production supervision by Sandra Grebenar and Ginger Boyer
Designed by Lydia D'moch

Little Whistle lived in Toytown, a wonderful place for a real guinea pig to be. All day long he slept in his cage, curled and warm, while children shopped for toys. Then at night, when the store was closed, he put on his blue pea coat and went to visit his friends.

His friends, of course, were toys. Toys are always toys when people are watching. But at night, when the shades are drawn, they walk and talk just like anyone else. Violet, the little china doll, sang like a bird. Rabbit ran like...well...a *rabbit*. Soldier read to the Toytown babies. Lion thought about vanilla cookies. And Bear tried on hats.

Little Whistle loved to ride the Toytown train and see them all.

Tonight he visited Soldier first. Soldier was reading to the babies and to a gorilla named Pete, who liked to hear stories, too. Pete was polite and quiet, and he made room for Little Whistle on the shelf.

When the story was over, the babies fell asleep.

"Soldier," Little Whistle whispered, so as not to wake them, "I think it is Christmastime."

"Yes," Soldier said with a salute. "The lights are twinkling."

"And the bells are jingling," said Pete.

"And children are talking of Santa," said Little Whistle.

"Santa?" asked Soldier. "Who is Santa?"

Lion jumped into a nearby tree. "Does he make vanilla cookies?"

"Does he make hats?" asked Bear.

"Does he like to run?" asked Rabbit as she went speeding by.

"He makes toys," sang Violet from the china-doll shelf. "Toys for all the children."

Little Whistle looked around at his friends.

"Did Santa make *you*?" he asked.

Soldier looked at Bear who looked at Violet who looked at Lion who looked at Pete who looked at Rabbit who had suddenly stopped running.

"I don't know who made me," said Rabbit. "I never thought about it."

"Nor I," said Soldier.

"Nor I," said Bear.

Everyone looked at Little Whistle.

"I guess my mother made me," said Little Whistle in a small voice.

The toys were very quiet. Lion looked especially sad.

"Well, *someone* made all of you!" said Little Whistle.

"Do *you* think it was Santa?" asked Bear.

"We will find out," said Little Whistle. "We will write Santa a letter."

"Yes!" said Pete. "There's a letter box by the front door."

"We'll ask Santa if *he* made us!" said Lion, already feeling much better. "I'm sure he did."

"Of course," said Soldier.

"Of course," said Rabbit.

"Of course," said Bear, taking off his sombrero and putting on a beret. "But we want to be sure."

Little Whistle found a nice piece of paper and a pen beside the register. Violet wrote the letter:

> *Dear Santa,*
> *Did you make us?*
> > *Your friends,*
> > *Violet, Soldier, Bear,*
> > *Lion, Pete, and Rabbit*

Pete put their letter in the letter box.

Every night, Little Whistle and his friends hoped for a letter from Santa. But none came.

"Do you think Santa will ever write back?" Lion asked.

Then one beautiful snowy night, when Toytown and all the world was especially quiet and peaceful, something wonderful happened.

Little Whistle and his friends were listening to Violet sing a Christmas song. The song was so lovely even Rabbit had stopped to listen.

When the song was over, everyone clapped and Rabbit was about to start running again. But there was a jingling at the door.

"What was that?" asked Little Whistle. He and his friends all rode the train to see.

There, beside the door, was a big shiny box with a note:

from **Santa**, who made YOU

And in the big shiny box were extra parts for every toy in the store. If someone needed a new nose, it was there. If a doll wanted new shoes, she found them. If a pirate had lost his parrot, the box gave him another. If a certain Lion loved vanilla cookies, he found a dozen. Every toy found just what was needed, and the box never grew empty. It gave and gave and gave.

Little Whistle felt so happy.

"Did you get anything, Little Whistle?" asked Soldier, who had a new book to read.

"I got a wonderful Christmas," said Little Whistle. "I don't need anything else."

But later that night, when the little guinea pig returned to his cage to sleep, he found tucked beside his log a small, beautiful blanket.

And he fell asleep beneath the stars.